The Little Germ Who Wants to Go Home

El pequeño germen que quiere regresar a casa

Lilia V. Guerrero
Ilustrado por Eleyna V. Guerrero

To past, present, and future Itsy Bitsy students.

ISBN: 978-0-578-72738-7

I'm scared!

¡Tengo miedo!

I'm **VERY** scared!

¡Tengo **MUCHO** miedo!

I want to go home!

¡Quiero regresar a casa!

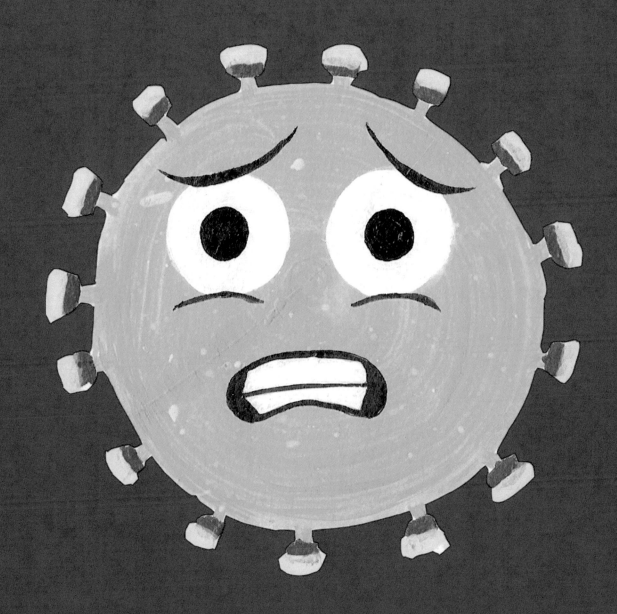

In case you haven't figured it out, I'm a little germ. I'm scared because I'm lost. I have a family and lots of friends who I miss. I need your help to get back home!

En caso que no lo hayas descubierto, soy un pequeño germen. Tengo miedo porque estoy perdido. Tengo una familia y muchos amigos que extraño.¡Necesito tu ayuda para regresar a casa!

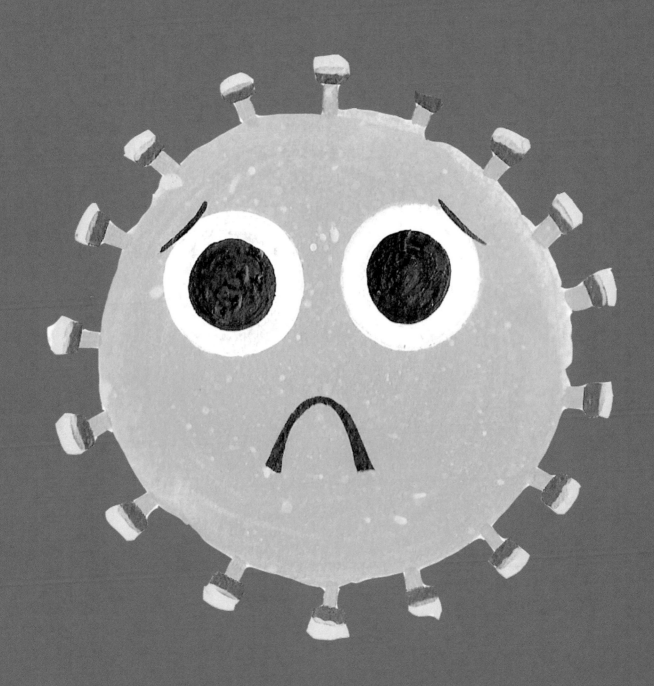

This morning I got stuck on a scary thing that had FIVE feet and NO face!
It looked something like this.

¡Esta mañana quedé atrapado en una cosa aterradora que tenía CINCO patas, pero NO tenía cara! Se veía así.

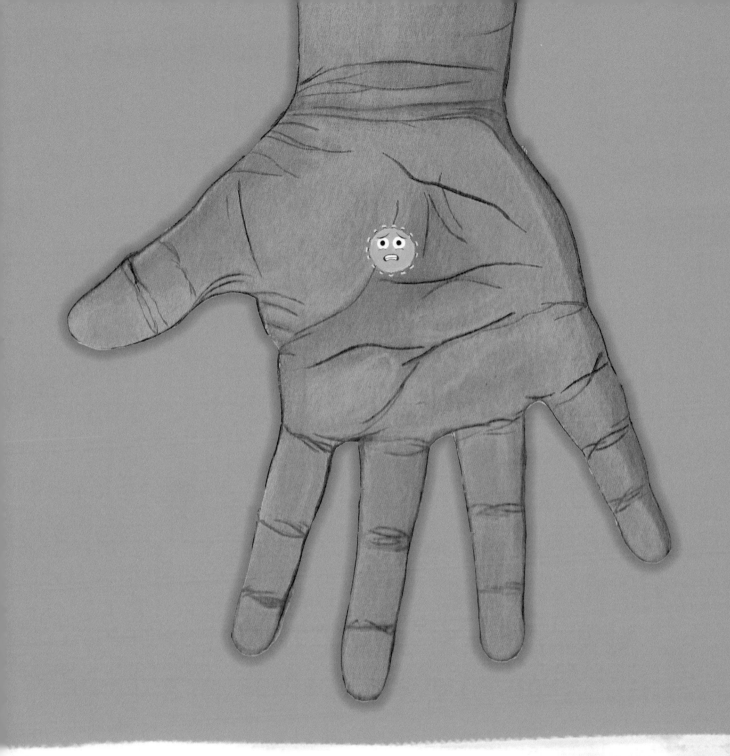

I tried to jump off, but I was afraid of hurting myself so I stayed stuck.

Traté de saltar, pero tenía miedo de lastimarme, así que me quedé atrapado.

The ugly thing grabbed something round and delicious so I jumped on it!

¡Esta cosa fea agarró algo delicioso y redondo, y salté sobre ella!

I thought that would be my ride home, but instead I ended up in something that looked like this.

Pensé que sería mi viaje a casa. En cambio, terminé en algo que se veía así.

I was afraid these big white things would crush me!

¡Tenía miedo de que las grandes cosas blancas me aplastaran!

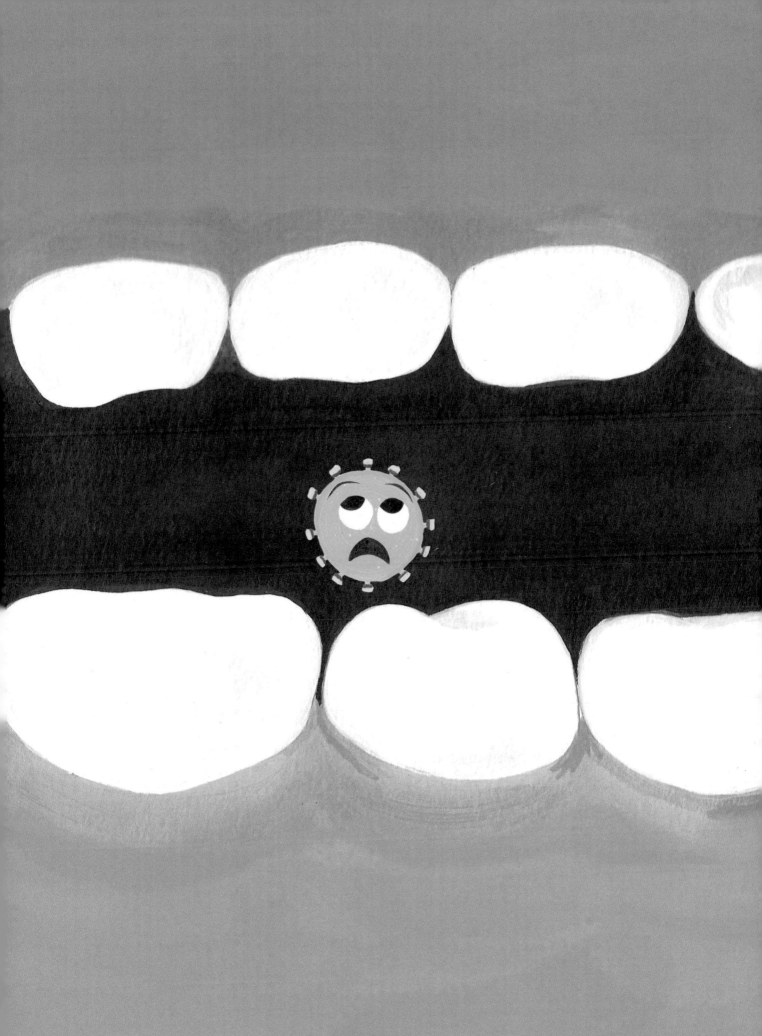

I got lucky because I am still in one piece.

Tuve suerte porque todavía estoy en una pieza.

Thank you for your help!
¡Gracias por tu ayuda!

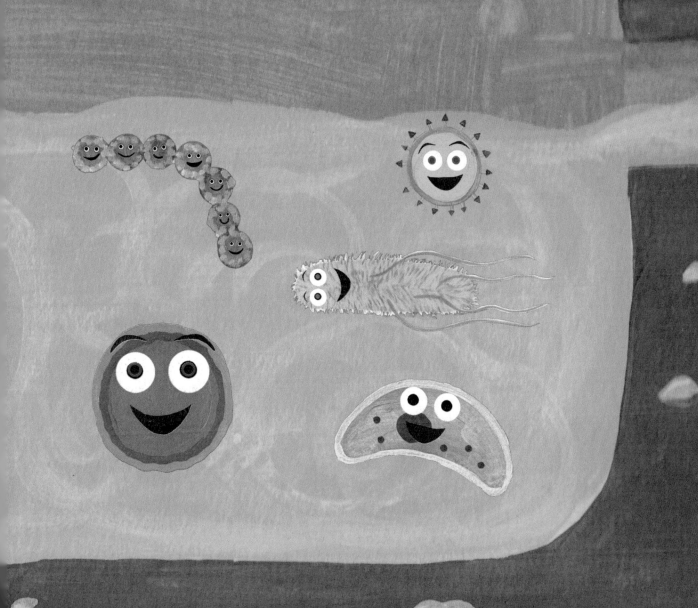

And just in case one of us gets stuck on you, always wash your hands! And please NEVER put your fingers in your mouth.

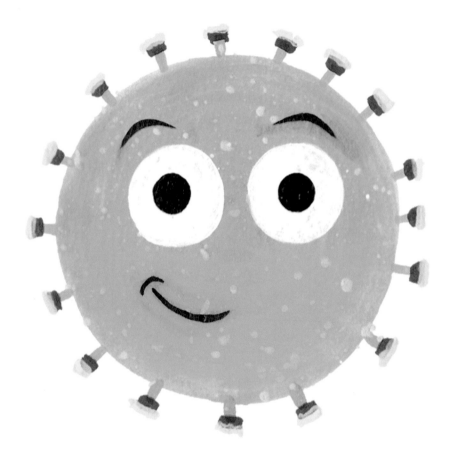

¡Y en caso de que alguno de nosotros se quede atrapado en ti, lávate siempre las manos!
Y por favor NUNCA te metas los dedos en la boca.

$10.95

ISBN 978-0-578-72738-7

51095>

9 780578 727387

This situation got even scarier! I was being pushed into a **dark** and **scary** tunnel!

I had to get out!

I WAS SO SCAAAARED!!!

¡Esta situación solo se volvió más aterradora! ¡Fuí empujado a un tunel y **aterricé** en un lugar **oscuro**!

¡Tenía que salir!

¡ESTABA ASUSTADO!

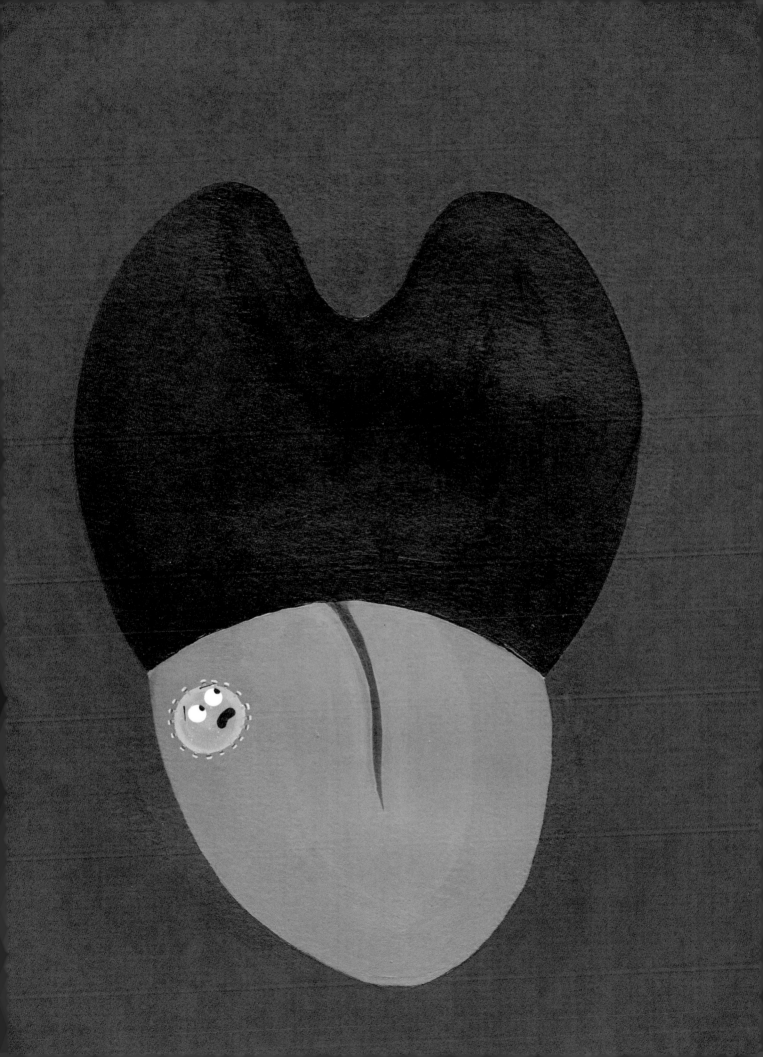

I started kicking and biting and hitting and screaming!

¡Empecé a patear y morder y golpear y gritar!

Suddenly, I heard a **BIG**.....

De repente, escuché un **GRAN** ...

And here I am back on this weird and scary thing again.

Y aquí estoy de vuelta en esta cosa extraña y aterradora.

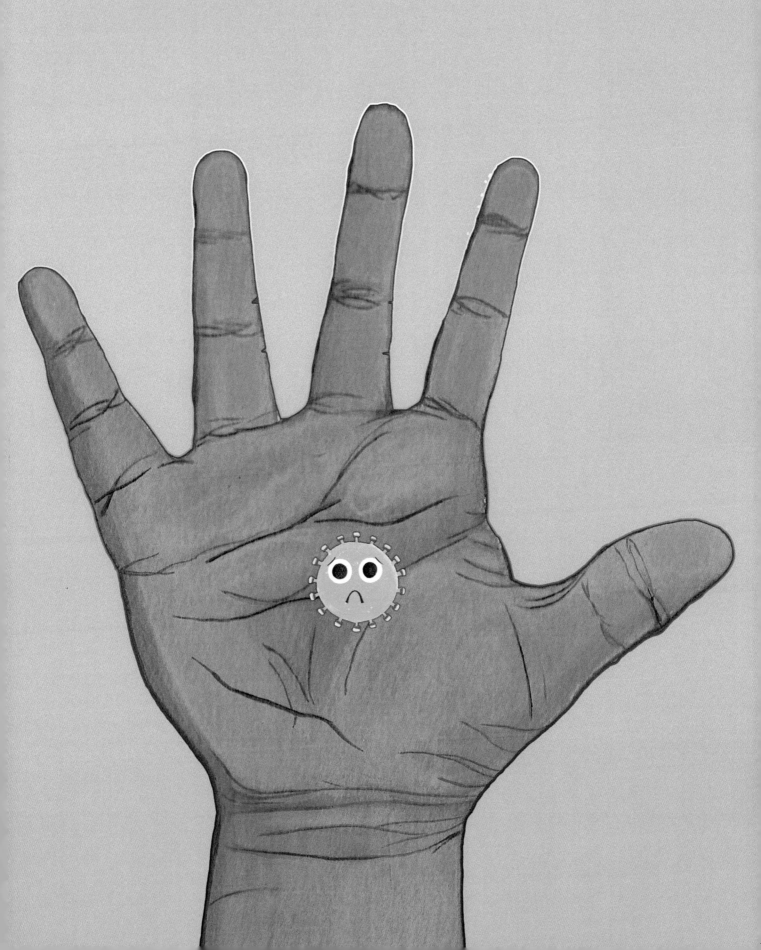

There is only one way for me to get back home.

Can you help me?

Solo hay una forma de regresar a casa.

¿Me puedes ayudar?

All we need is soap

Solo necesitamos

jabón

and

y

water.

agua.

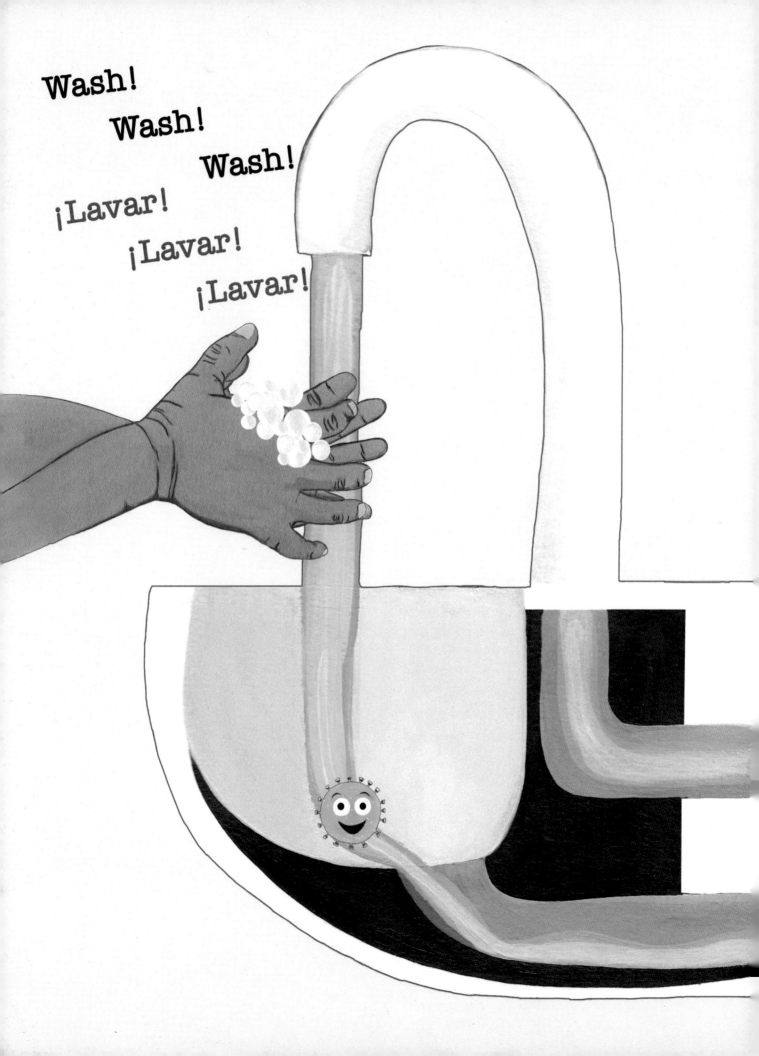

Home again!
¡De nuevo en casa!

Made in the USA
Monee, IL
05 September 2020